The Usborne
First
Encyclopedia
of
Space

Paul Dowswell

Designed by Keith Newell & Helen Wood

Illustrated by Gary Bines & David Hancock

Space consultant: Stuart Atkinson
Managing designer: Mary Cartwright
Managing editor: Felicity Brooks
Digital manipulation: John Russell, Mike Olley & Roger Bolton
Picture research: Ruth King
Cover design: Laura Fearn

Using Internet links

There are lots of exciting places on the Internet where you can find out about space. This book contains descriptions of Web sites that you can visit by clicking on links on the Usborne Quicklinks Web site. Just go to **www.usborne-quicklinks.com** and enter the keywords "first space". Here are some of the things you can do on the Web sites described in this book:

- Take a virtual tour of the Solar System.

- Find out how astronauts train for space flights.

- Watch a movie about the Big Bang.

- See amazing pictures taken from space.

Safety on the Internet

Here are a few simple rules to help keep you safe while you are online:

- Ask your parent's or guardian's permission before you connect to the Internet.

- Never give out information about yourself, such as your real name, address or phone number.

- Never arrange to meet someone you started talking to on the Internet.

- If a site asks you to log in or register by typing your name or e-mail address, ask permission from an adult first.

- If you receive an e-mail from someone you don't know, tell an adult. Don't reply to it.

Downloadable pictures

Pictures in this book that have the ★ symbol next to them can be downloaded from Usborne Quicklinks and printed out free of charge, for use in homework or projects. The pictures must not be copied or distributed for any commercial purpose. To find the pictures, go to **www.usborne-quicklinks.com** and follow the simple instructions there.

Site availability

The links in Usborne Quicklinks are regularly updated, but occasionally, you may get a message that a site is unavailable. This might be temporary, so try again later. If any of the sites close down, we will, if possible, replace them with alternatives. You will find an up-to-date list of sites in Usborne Quicklinks.

What you need

Most of the Web sites listed in this book can be accessed using a standard home computer and a Web browser (the software that lets you look at information from the Internet). Some sites need extra programs (plug-ins) to play sound or show videos or animations. If you go to a site and do not have the necessary plug-in, a message will come up on the screen. There is usually a button on the site that you can click on to download the plug-in. Alternatively, go to Usborne Quicklinks and click on **Net Help**. There, you can find links to download plug-ins.

Notes for parents

The Web sites described in this book are regularly reviewed and the links in Usborne Quicklinks are updated. However, the content of a Web site may change at any time and Usborne Publishing is not responsible for the content on any Web site other than its own. We recommend that children are supervised while on the Internet, that they do not use Internet Chat Rooms, and that you use Internet filtering software to block unsuitable material. Please ensure that your children read and follow the safety guidelines printed on the left. For more information, see the **Net Help** area on the Usborne Quicklinks Web site.

A COMPUTER IS NOT ESSENTIAL TO USE THIS BOOK

This book is a complete, superb, self-contained information book by itself.

Contents

Amazing space

Space is full of amazing sights. Some you can see with your own eyes, or with a telescope or binoculars. Others can only be seen using special equipment. Here are some of the things you can find out about in this book.

Spacecraft

Rockets have been going into space for the last 40 years. They have taken people as far as the Moon, and spacecraft without people in them have visited distant planets such as Uranus and Neptune.

This American rocket is taking three people to the Moon.

Astronauts

People who travel into space are called astronauts. They have to train for many years before their trip.

This astronaut wears a space suit to "walk" in space. ★

Stars

A star is a blazing ball of very hot gas. The Sun is a star.

Below you can see new stars being made from clouds of dust.

The planet
Neptune

Moons

Most planets have
moons. These are
mini-planets
which travel
around other
planets.

This is Io, one of
Jupiter's moons.

Planets

A planet is an enormous ball of rock or
gas which travels around a star. A group
of planets moving around a star is known
as a solar system.

The planet Saturn

Comets

Comets are balls of dirty
ice, which fly around in
space. Sometimes
they crash into planets.

This is
a comet. ★

Galaxies

Galaxies are huge groups of stars. Our
Sun and its solar system is in a galaxy
called the Milky Way. Scientists think
there are billions of galaxies in space.

This galaxy is called
the Sombrero Galaxy.
It has millions of stars.

The moving sky

Everything in the Universe, from little moons to entire solar systems and galaxies, is moving. Even if you are sitting very still to read this book, you are still moving through space at 1,000km (600 miles) a second.

Spinners

All planets and moons spin around. Earth spins at roughly 1,600kmph (1,000mph). It takes 24 hours to go all the way around. We measure our day by this amount of time.

This photo of stars was made over several hours. The position of the stars has changed in the sky because the Earth is spinning around.

Night and day

As Earth turns, the part that faces the Sun is lit up, and the part that faces away from the Sun is dark. This is why we have day and night.

It is still dark in North America.

1

7:00am Sun rises over Europe.

Sun is rising in North America.

2

12:00 noon Sun is high in the sky in Europe.

The Earth keeps turning as it travels around the Sun. It takes 365 days (one year) to go once around the Sun.

3

7:00pm Sun has gone down in Europe.

Sun is high in the sky in North America.

Big circles

As they spin, planets and moons move through space in huge circular paths called orbits. It is hard to see them moving as they seem to travel slowly, like the hour hand on a watch.

The yellow lines and arrows in the pictures on the right show the paths a planet and a moon take in their orbits.

A planet orbits around a sun.

A moon orbits around a planet.

Gravity

Planets stay in orbit around the Sun, instead of flying off into space, because of a force called gravity.

Everything in the Universe is held together by gravity. It pulls every object toward every other object.

Path of Earth's orbit

The Earth stays in orbit around the Sun, held there by gravity.

The Sun's force of gravity pulls on the Earth and stops it from flying off into space.

Sun's force of gravity

If the planets and moons in our Solar System did not move, they would all crash into the Sun.

Sun

Telescopes

Telescopes make things look bigger. Ever since they were invented 400 years ago, astronomers have been using them to find out more about space.

How a telescope works

A telescope uses a curved glass circle called a lens to magnify (make larger) objects. The first astronomer to use a telescope was an Italian man named Galileo. His telescope made stars and planets look three times bigger.

A replica of Galileo's telescope

Lens

Lens

Light comes in here.

Hollow tube

Galileo used a telescope to discover rings around Saturn.

Modern telescopes

Today, astronomers use curved mirrors in telescopes, as well as glass lenses. These give better images. Big astronomy telescopes are placed high on mountains. The air is clearer there, so there is a better view of the sky.

This is the Kitt Peak Observatory in Arizona, USA.

The telescope inside this tower is called the Mayall Telescope. It is one of the biggest in the world. It looks at distant galaxies and nebulas.

Go to **www.usborne-quicklinks.com** and type in the keywords "first space" for a link to a Web site where you can see amazing photographs taken by the Hubble Space Telescope.

Space telescope

A big telescope called the Hubble Space Telescope orbits the Earth. It is outside the haze and pollution of our planet's atmosphere*, so it is able to take incredibly clear photographs of the Universe.

Antenna

The telescope can be moved around to point at different parts of the sky.

This lid protects the lens when the telescope isn't being used.

The Hubble Space Telescope

The Hubble Telescope has two solar panels. They use energy from the Sun to make electricity to power the telescope.

Cameras here take pictures of what Hubble can see.

Two radio antennae send pictures back to Earth.

Antenna

Solar panel

Solar panel

Space repairs

When the Hubble Space Telescope was first put into space in 1990 it didn't work properly. Three years later, some astronauts went up in a space shuttle to repair it. Now the telescope sends back very clear pictures.

Hubble Telescope

Astronauts
Space shuttle

*See page 29 for more about Earth's atmosphere.

9

Radio telescopes

In space there are billions of things that are too dark or far away for an ordinary telescope to look at.

A radio telescope can find things an ordinary telescope can't. This is because it does not use light to "see".

Star signals

Stars and other space objects all give off some kind of signal which shows that they are there. This may be light, heat or sound. It may also be another type of signal called a radio wave. This is what a radio telescope picks up.

This is a galaxy called Centaurus A. Like all galaxies it is giving off radio waves which travel through space.

A radio telescope picks up these radio waves. It sends them to a computer, to be turned into a picture. ★

This is a computer picture of radio waves from Centaurus A.

Radio waves

Unlike light telescopes, radio telescopes can be used during the day as well as at night.

Radio waves

The radio waves that stars give off are similar to the signals your radio at home picks up. But if you listened to them, you would hear a crackling, whooshing noise, rather than any voices or music.

The Very Large Array

These radio telescopes are in New Mexico, USA. There are 27 dishes in a group called the Very Large Array. Each one can be used on its own or with the other 26 dishes, to sweep over a huge part of the sky.

This is how big a man looks in comparison with a dish.

Each one of these dishes is 25m (80ft) wide.

Trips into space

People have only been sending rockets into space since 1957. Before then, rockets fell back to the ground before they could reach space. They were not powerful enough to escape Earth's gravity.

The space shuttle

The first people went into space in 1961. Since then hundreds of men and women have followed them. Today, astronauts fly into space in a rocket called a space shuttle. This is how it works.

Tailfin

When it returns from space, the shuttle's wings help it to glide back to Earth.

Astronauts have to wear spacesuits to go into the cargo bay or outside the space shuttle.

USA

NASA Endeavour

Booster rocket

Fuel tank

1. Shuttle blasts off from Earth.

2. Two booster rockets fall away when their fuel runs out, and parachute back to Earth.

3. Main engine takes shuttle into space. Big fuel tank falls away when it is empty.

A new spacecraft?

When they have enough money, American scientists will build a new type of shuttle. It will make space travel cheaper than it is now. ★

This robot arm is putting a space telescope into orbit.

The pilot sits here.

Seven people can live on the shuttle. They can stay in space for several days.

Cargo bay

Can you see a sleeping astronaut?

The big cargo bay can carry telescopes, satellites or parts of a space station.

The crew compartment in the shuttle is on two levels. At the top is the flight deck, where the pilot flies the craft. Below, there is space for the rest of the crew to do experiments and rest.

4. On its return, the shuttle glides back though Earth's atmosphere. ★

5. Shuttle touches down. It lands on wheels like a plane.

NASA United States Discovery

Go to **www.usborne-quicklinks.com** and type in the keywords "first space" for a link to a Web site where you can watch videos of space shuttles in action.

Astronaut training

Astronauts train for years to prepare for a trip into space. Here you can see some of the ways they do this at an astronaut training school in Houston, Texas, USA.

Which button do I press?

A space shuttle pilot steers the spaceship from a control panel which looks like the one below. There are hundreds of buttons to press. Astronauts learn how to control a shuttle in a machine called a flight simulator.

Flight simulator

Astronauts sit in here.

The cabin moves around like a real space shuttle.

This is what it looks like ★ inside a flight simulator. Television screens show what the real view would be like.

An astronaut learning to repair a satellite

Astronauts train in a huge pool which is 7.6m (25ft) deep.

Floating around

In space everything floats. This is called being weightless and it is a very strange feeling. Astronauts get used to it by training under water, which is the nearest thing on Earth to being weightless.

Here is an astronaut doing a space walk under water.

Go to **www.usborne-quicklinks.com** and type in the keywords "first space" for a link to a Web site packed with information about how astronauts train.

Making a quick escape

Astronauts must learn how to get out of their space shuttle quickly during an emergency at take-off or landing. Here you can see an astronaut trying out an escape when the shuttle has landed back on Earth.

This astronaut is sliding down a rope to escape from the space shuttle.

Robot arm

This is a full-scale model of the space shuttle's cargo bay. This is where astronauts learn to use the shuttle's robot arm, which moves satellites in or out of the cargo bay.

Divers help the astronauts if they get into trouble.

Taking the "Vomit Comet"

Astronauts can also learn how it feels to be weightless by flying in a jet which takes a steep climb. At the top of the climb they are weightless for 30 seconds. People feel sick sometimes, so the plane is nicknamed the "Vomit Comet".

The plane has to climb very steeply and then take a dive for the astronauts to feel weightless inside it.

★

Here are astronauts floating aound in the plane. There is lots of padding to stop them from getting hurt.

15

A walk in space

Space is deadly. There is no air to breathe, so outside a spacecraft, an astronaut must wear an outfit called a spacesuit to stay alive. Spacesuits are like body-size spaceships, with their own air and water supplies.

A camera on the helmet films what the astronaut is doing.

A spacesuit has several very thin but strong layers. These protect the astronaut from tiny meteoroids, and the heat and cold of space.

Because his face is hidden by his helmet, this stripe shows other astronauts who is in this spacesuit.

Lights on the helmet help the astronaut to see in the dark.

The astronaut can control the equipment in a spacesuit from this unit.

The suit is flexible enough to allow easy movement.

Walk to work

Astronauts make space walks to repair satellites, build space stations or check the outside of their spaceships. On these pages you can see two American astronauts making a space walk from their space shuttle in 1997.

Go to **www.usborne-quicklinks.com** and type in the keywords "first space" for a link to a Web site describing the history of human spaceflight.

Survival equipment

Here is some of the equipment astronauts need to stay alive and comfortable outside their spaceships. Sometimes space walks can last for five hours or more.

★

The shiny visor of the helmet protects against blinding, bright sunlight.

★

This cap holds a radio microphone and ear piece in place.

★

A drink bag has a tube which goes straight to the astronaut's mouth.

★

This is the "Primary Life Support System". It contains air for the astronaut to breathe.

★

This outfit is worn next to the body. It has tubes of water which the astronaut can make hot or cold, to warm up or cool down.

★

Padded gloves have rubber fingertips so the astronaut can feel things more easily.

Boiling and freezing

When astronauts on a space walk face the Sun, its rays are hotter than boiling water. But when their spaceships travel around the dark side of the Earth, temperatures drop way below freezing.

A space shuttle takes 90 minutes to go around the Earth.

45 minutes in darkness

45 minutes in sunlight

Living in space

Space stations are homes in space where astronauts can look at the Earth and do experiments. People can live in them for many months at a time. The first space station was set up over 30 years ago.

The future

Here is what a space station of the future may look like. This one is called the International Space Station (ISS). It is being built now, and could look like this when it is finished. Seven or more people could live or work here. A space shuttle will take them up here, and back to Earth.

This is the inside of a laboratory where scientists can do tests to see how things behave in space.

★

These are solar panels. They make energy by collecting heat from the Sun, and turning it into electricity.

Go to **www.usborne-quicklinks.com** and type in the keywords "first space" for a link to a Web site where you can take a tour of the International Space Station.

Radio antennae and dishes send signals to and from the Earth.

Criss-cross steel tubes hold the station together.

The station floats 400km (250 miles) above the Earth.

There are 16 different layers in the walls. They keep heat or cold out, and stop meteorites from getting in.

Crew members live here and carry out experiments.

This tiny spacecraft could take the crew back to Earth if anything went wrong.

Living area

The living area is where the crew will go when they are not working. Below is one idea of what this might look like. Because there is no gravity in space they will float around inside it, and will not need chairs to sit on, or beds to lie in.

Space toilet

This is what a space toilet looks like. It is quite tricky to use.

★ Handles for the astronaut to hold onto

Seat

Air sucks waste through this tube.

Urine is cleaned and turned back into water. Solid waste is frozen and returned to Earth.

★ Level three
The crew can exercise here.

Level two
Sleeping area. Each person has a small, private space.

Level one
The crew can eat together around this big table.

Dangers and disasters

Going into space can be very dangerous. Astronauts only survive because their spaceship or spacesuit protects them. The most dangerous parts of the journey are the take-off, and return to Earth.

When the space shuttle Challenger's main fuel tank caught fire, it caused this massive explosion.

Shuttle explosion

One of the worst ever space disasters happened in 1986. A space shuttle named Challenger exploded only 90 seconds after taking off. All seven of the astronauts on board the shuttle died.

The Challenger space shuttle taking off

Fuel leaking from here caught fire.

Go to **www.usborne-quicklinks.com** and type in the keywords "first space" for a link to a Web site where you can find out more about what happened to the Apollo 13 mission.

Lucky Apollo 13

In 1970, three astronauts were going to the Moon in a spacecraft named Apollo 13. Halfway there, part of the spacecraft blew up. Some of the fuel supply had exploded. The crew survived the disaster, but almost ran out of air on the way back to Earth.

An explosion here nearly destroyed Apollo 13.

The astronauts escaped into this part of Apollo 13.

One whole side of the spaceship blew away.

The astronauts made this box from storage bags, tape and air hoses to clean their air.

Up in smoke

The European Space Agency launched its first Ariane 5 rocket in 1996. But a computer on board did not work properly. Less than a minute after take-off, Ariane 5 began to fly in the wrong direction. Then it broke into pieces and exploded.

Ariane 5 taking off

Satellites and space probes

Satellites and space probes are spaceships with no people in them. Instead, scientists control them from Earth. Most satellites and probes have cameras or other kinds of viewing equipment.

This is the European Remote Sensing Satellite, known as ERS. It can take very detailed pictures of the Earth.

Satellites

Some satellites look down on Earth and others look out into space. Other types of satellites are used to carry television pictures or phone messages around the world. ★

Solar panels

This is the SOHO satellite, which looks at the atmosphere of the Sun. It is also used to find out about the solar wind (see page 32).

Go to **www.usborne-quicklinks.com** and type in the keywords "first space" for a link to a Web site where you can learn more about satellites and build your own online.

Space probes

Space probes do similar jobs to satellites, but instead of orbiting the Earth, they visit other planets. All the planets have been visited, apart from Pluto. Sometimes space probes even land on other planets.

The painting on the right shows the Voyager space probe heading toward Neptune in 1989.

Space views

Here are two pictures taken by satellites. Special cameras are used to show particular details, which can also be made clearer with computers.

This ERS picture shows a hole in Antarctica's atmosphere.

This SOHO picture shows the outer edge of the Sun's surface.

A big picture

A satellite named COBE took the picture below. It is a temperature map of the entire universe.

Some parts of space are hotter than others. The red and blue areas show different temperatures.

COBE satellite

Into the future

Going into space is very expensive, so what happens in the future depends on how much money countries want to spend on exploring space. Here are some of the things that might happen over the next hundred years.

Spaceships such as this could visit Mars then return to Earth.

Mission to Mars

Space probes have landed on Mars, taken pictures and carried out experiments. There are now plans for a robot spaceship to visit the planet and return to Earth with samples of soil and rock. People could visit Mars within 20 years, if there is enough money for the trip. Space bases may be built there too, in about 50 years time.

A base on Mars might look like this.

Space tourists

The first tourist went into space in April 2001. Many other people would love to visit space too. In 20 years time it may be possible to spend a week in a hotel orbiting our planet. Space tourists can feel what it's like to be weightless, and see stunning views of Earth.

A hotel in space might look like this.

Shuttle bringing people back to Earth

A lift into orbit

A very cheap way to get people and equipment into space could be a giant elevator. It sounds impossible, but it could be built with new materials which are 100 times stronger than steel. ★

The elevator would need to be 200km (125 miles) high.

Asteroid watch

Scientists are watching the skies for any asteroids that might be heading for Earth. A big one could wipe out life on our planet. If an asteroid is spotted, in the future it might be possible to destroy it or send it off course.

This picture shows what an asteroid hitting the Earth might look like.

Is anyone out there?

Ever since people first began to study the stars, they have wondered whether there is life in space. At the moment we don't know. Some astronomers think we will find evidence of alien life before the end of the century.

Reaching out

Two kinds of space probes are heading out of our Solar System. Pioneer probes carry a picture of people and a map that shows where Earth is. Voyagers carry a disc with sounds and pictures of Earth. These are to show any alien who may find them what we look like.

Pioneer probe ★

Voyager probe ★

The Voyager disc

The Pioneer map and picture

New planets

Recently, astronomers have discovered planets in orbit around some stars. Perhaps there may be life there. Radio telescopes, such as the ones at Arecibo in Puerto Rico (shown below), and Jodrell Bank in England, search the skies around these planets, for evidence of alien signals.

Arecibo radio telescope is the largest in the world.

Go to **www.usborne-quicklinks.com** and type in the keywords "first space" for a link to a Web site where you can find out how to search for alien life.

Life on Europa?

Europa, one of Jupiter's moons, has an icy surface. Under it there may be a cold, dark sea. Scientists think they may find simple creatures there, perhaps like those that live deep under water on Earth. A space probe will visit Europa in the future to try to find out more about it.

Europa

In the future submarine probes from Earth may explore under the ice of Europa.

What might aliens look like ?

If we do find life in space, it may not be very interesting. It could be slime or moss, rather than intelligent creatures with arms, legs and heads, like us.

Aliens may look like this in films, but we don't really know what they might look like.
★

Some scientists think germ-like blobs found in a rock from Mars show life existed there.

What's in our Solar System?

Our Solar System is the Sun and everything that revolves around it. It includes all the planets and their moons, and space objects such as comets. There are also two vast bands of drifting rocks called the Asteroid Belt and the Kuiper Belt.

In this picture of the Solar System the planets are not shown to scale.

Comets fly around the Solar System.

Days and years

A day is the time it takes for a planet to spin around once. Earth's day lasts 24 hours. A year is the time it takes for a planet to go all the way around the Sun. Earth's year lasts for 365 days.

Earth

Sun

A day   A year

Asteroid Belt

Saturn is the second biggest planet.

Neptune is a gas planet, like Jupiter, Saturn, and Uranus. The gas planets are all much bigger than the rocky planets in our Solar System.

Go to **www.usborne-quicklinks.com** and type in the keywords "first space" for a link to a Web site where you can take an incredible tour of the Solar System.

Moons

All the planets in the Solar System have at least one moon, apart from Mercury and Venus. The moons orbit their planets, and are held in place by gravity.

Jupiter is the biggest planet.

Venus

Mercury

The Sun

Mars

Earth

Atmosphere

Most planets have an atmosphere – a layer of gas that covers the surface. Earth's atmosphere is made of air. It stretches 400km (250 miles) above us. It provides air to breathe, and protects us from the Sun's heat.

Earth's atmosphere

Uranus spins on its side. It has rings like Saturn.

Pluto is a tiny, rocky planet.

Beyond Pluto lies a band of icy rocks named the Kuiper Belt.

The Moon

The Moon travels around the Earth, just like the Earth travels around the Sun. So far, the Moon is the only part of the Solar System that people have been able to visit.

Sea of Crises

The Moon's "seas" are actually dark patches of melted rock.

Sea of Tranquility

Craters were made by rocks from space, crashing into the Moon.

Sea of Serenity

Apollo 15 landed here in 1971.

Sea of Rain

Earth

If you were orbiting the Moon in a spaceship, this is how far away Earth would look.

When people went to the Moon between 1969 and 1972, it took their spaceships three days to get there.

What is the Moon like?

The Moon is very different from Earth. There is no air, no weather, and no life. It is a dreary, dusty place that is boiling hot by day and freezing at night. The surface is covered with saucer-shaped holes called craters. You can see some if you look at the Moon on a clear night. Some are so huge, a city the size of London could fit inside them.

Go to **www.usborne-quicklinks.com** and type in the keywords "first space" for a link to a Web site where you can find out more about missions to the moon.

Where did the Moon come from?

The Moon is about the same age as the Earth. Here is one idea about where it came from.

1. Soon after the Earth formed, a planet hit it. ★

2. Rocks broke off and shot into space. ★

3. The rocks were held in ★ orbit by Earth's gravity.

4. These rocks slowly formed into the Moon. ★

Moon facts

● The Moon does not give out any of its own light. We can only see it because the Sun shines on it.

● The Moon takes 27 days to spin around once, and 27 days to go all the way around the Earth too.

● We never see one side of the Moon, because it is always facing away from us.

Moon landings

People have visited the Moon six times, but no one has been there since 1972. The spaceships that landed on the Moon each carried two astronauts. They stayed for up to three days before returning.

This photo shows the Apollo 15 Moon landing. You can see where they are on the Moon, on the opposite page.

This spaceship is called a lunar module.

The astronaut is saluting the American flag.

The astronauts used a car powered by electricity.

UNITED STATES

The Sun

The Sun is a star. It is a huge ball of blazing gas that makes vast amounts of light and heat which we call sunshine. It is so big it could hold a million planets the size of Earth. It looks like it is burning, but it is actually exploding like a massive bomb.

The size of the Earth, compared to the Sun

The Sun's surface is called the photosphere. The temperature there is 5,500°C (10,000°F).

Dark areas on the Sun are called sunspots. The temperature is lower there.

The solar wind

As well as light and heat, the Sun also sends out a stream of invisible specks, called particles, into space. This is called the solar wind. When the particles pass by the North and South Poles of Earth they can make the air glow beautiful reds, blues, greens and purples.

This is the solar wind lighting up the sky near the North Pole.

This is a solar prominence. It is a massive arch of hot gas, which reaches out into space like a huge flaming tongue.

Solar surface

The Sun makes sunlight by burning four million tonnes (tons) of fuel every second. You can see in this picture that its surface is a churning mass of explosions. Solar flares and fiery loops of gas leap out into space.

The photo on the right shows a close-up of the Sun's surface. You can see jets of gas called plasma loops.

Liquid, ice or gas?

Life exists on Earth because our planet is the right distance from the Sun for water to be a liquid, rather than ice or a gas.

Mars is too cold.

Venus is too hot.

Sun

Earth is just right.

★

Sometimes, white areas appear on the surface of the Sun. These are called faculae. The temperature here is even higher than that of the rest of the Sun.

Mercury and Venus

Mercury and Venus are the two planets closest to the Sun. Both of them are small and very hot. Mercury has almost no atmosphere, but Venus is covered with a thick layer of gas.

Tiny Mercury

Mercury is a tiny planet. Billions of years ago many rocks crashed into it, so its surface is covered with lots of craters. Because it is so close to the Sun, it has the shortest year of any planet. Mercury takes just 88 Earth days to travel around the Sun.

Mercury is a third the size of Earth, but is almost as heavy. It has a core of dense metal. This makes up nearly three-quarters of its inside.

Crust

Mercury

Metal core

Four billion years ago a huge meteorite hit Mercury. It made a massive crater called the Caloris Basin. This is more than 1,250km (800 miles) across.

★

Meteorite hitting Mercury

Go to **www.usborne-quicklinks.com** and type in the keywords "first space" for links to two Web sites where you can see amazing close-up pictures of Mercury and Venus.

Sweltering Venus

Venus is the nearest planet to us. Although it is farther away from the Sun than Mercury, its surface is actually hotter. This is because it has a thick atmosphere of the gas carbon dioxide. This atmosphere traps the Sun's heat and stops it from escaping back into space.

The picture below shows what the planet Venus looks like beneath its cloudy cover.

Different shades have been added here, to show the surface more clearly.

The picture below was taken by the Magellan probe. You can see some of the mountains and canyons on the surface of Venus.

The Magellan probe visited Venus between 1990 and 1994.

Mars

If you were standing on Mars, being there would be a little like being on Earth. There is a bright sky during the day, and you could see thin clouds, morning mists and light frosts. But Mars is a lot colder than our planet.

Mars in detail

Mars is half the size of Earth. It is mainly covered with rocks and dust. Most of it looks like a great big desert. It has a thin atmosphere of poisonous gas.

This is a polar ice cap, similar to the North Pole on Earth. Water here has frozen into a huge field of ice.

These marks are great fields of dark dust. They are blown around by fierce storms.

This is a volcano called Olympus Mons.

This is a volcano called Ascraeus Mons.

This is a huge canyon called The Valles Marineris.

★

The Viking 1 space probe visited Mars in 1976. It sent down the first craft to land on the surface.

Go to **www.usborne-quicklinks.com** and type in the keywords "first space" for a link to a Web site where you can find out more about missions to Mars and see some incredible photographs.

Volcanoes and canyons

Mars has some very interesting features. There are several volcanoes. The biggest one is called Olympus Mons. It is the largest in the Solar System. It rises 25km (15 miles) above the surface of Mars. There are also huge canyons and dried-up water channels.

Channels

The Olympus Mons volcano seen by a visiting space probe.

The Valles Marineris canyon is a huge crack along one side of the planet. It is so long it would stretch across the whole of the USA.

Astronomers think that channels like this were made by running water, which has now frozen or leaked away.

Visitors to Mars

The photograph below shows the surface of Mars. It was taken by the Pathfinder space probe, which landed there in 1997. On board was a little mobile robot called Sojourner. It carried TV cameras and could be moved around by scientists on Earth.

Scientists think that the rocks you can see in this picture were left here by a big flood, billions of years ago.

The Sojourner robot is the size of a microwave oven. This picture shows some of its more important features:
Ⓐ Solar panels make power from sunlight.
Ⓑ Small wheels with studded rims grip the surface.
Ⓒ Radio antenna keeps the robot in contact with Earth.
Ⓓ A camera and laser are used to help steer the robot.

Swirly world

Jupiter is the biggest planet in the Solar System. It also has the shortest day. It takes only 9 hours and 50 minutes to spin all the way around. It is a stormy planet. Swirling clouds of gas race around it, in great dark and light bands.

The Great Red Spot is a huge storm three times the size of Earth.

A pod from the Galileo space probe parachuted into Jupiter's gassy atmosphere in 1995.

Jupiter's moons

Jupiter has 50 moons. One of them, Ganymede, is the biggest moon in the Solar System. Another, named Io, has many volcanoes on its surface.

This space probe photograph shows thick, hot gas erupting from one of Io's volcanoes.

Go to **www.usborne-quicklinks.com** and type in the keywords "first space" for links to two Web sites where you can discover fun facts about Jupiter and Saturn and find out how to spot them in the night sky.

Ring world

Saturn is the second biggest planet in the Solar System. Many broad rings of rock and ice orbit around it. Saturn is very light. If you could put it in a huge swimming pool, it would float there.

All shapes and sizes

The rocks in Saturn's rings may have come from one of its moons. You can see what might have happened below. Some rocks in the rings are as big as a house, others are smaller than a pebble.

A moon collided with a planet.

It broke into billions of pieces.

The pieces stayed in Saturn's orbit.

Eventually, they formed Saturn's rings.

Saturn's moons

Saturn has at least 24 moons, and there may be more. Titan is the largest. It has a thick atmosphere.

Here you can see how big Titan is compared to the planet Mercury and our Moon.

The planet Mercury

Earth's Moon

Titan

This picture shows what Titan's atmosphere may look like, close up.

Uranus and Neptune

Uranus and Neptune are huge gas planets. Both are around four times bigger than Earth.

They are difficult to spot in the night sky, but you can see them with a telescope.

Uranus

Neptune

Earth

This is how big Uranus and Neptune are compared to the Earth.

Uranus

This world spins on its side. Its outer surface is cloaked by a thin mist, which wraps around a thick gassy surface. Further inside, Uranus has a core of solid rock.

Here are some of Uranus's moons.

Umbriel

Ariel

Titania

Oberon

Miranda

Puzzle Moon

Uranus has 21 moons. One of them, Miranda, looks like a huge jigsaw puzzle. Perhaps, millions of years ago, it broke into pieces. Gradually time and gravity put it back together.

★
A comet may have crashed into Miranda.

★
Miranda's pieces drifted together.

★
Miranda slowly put itself back in one piece.

This is what the surface of Miranda looks like now.

Go to **www.usborne-quicklinks.com** and type in the keywords "first space" for links to two Web sites where you can find out how Uranus and Neptune were first discovered and how they got their names.

Neptune

Neptune has the worst storms in the Solar System. Winds of 2,000kmph (1,250mph) whip clouds of methane around the planet.

Spouting moon

Neptune has eight moons. One, named Triton, is a frozen world. Ice on its surface acts like a greenhouse, magnifying the Sun's feeble rays, and heating gas that lies beneath. This causes hot jets of gas and slush to spout out through the ice and into space.

Triton orbits in the opposite direction from all of Neptune's other moons.

Visitor from Earth

Uranus and Neptune were visited by the Voyager 2 space probe in 1986 and 1989. The probe took 12 years to get to Neptune from Earth.

This picture shows what the surface of Triton might look like. A jet of gas and slush is spouting out from beneath the ice.

Voyager 2 space probe

Pluto and beyond

Pluto lies at the very edge of the Solar System, nearly six billion km (four billion miles) away from the Sun. Pluto is so far away it was only discovered in 1930. Unlike the gassy planets Uranus and Neptune, Pluto is a solid ball of rock and ice.

Moon-sized

Pluto is a tiny planet. It is smaller than our Moon. Both Pluto, and its moon Charon, could fit into the borders of the USA. Some astronomers think Pluto is an asteroid, and not a planet. ★

Pluto's moon, Charon.

Pluto

A space probe would take 12 years to get to Pluto.

Pluto may have a thin atmosphere of nitrogen gas.

Go to **www.usborne-quicklinks.com** and type in the keywords "first space" for a link to a Web site with amazing facts about Pluto, an interactive puzzle and a quiz to test your knowledge.

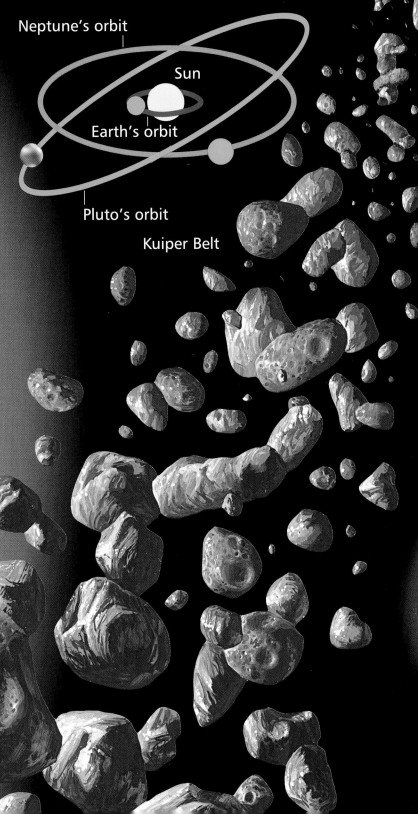

Odd orbit

Pluto takes 248 Earth years to go around the Sun. For 20 of these years it is closer to the Sun than Neptune. While all the other planets orbit on roughly the same level, Pluto spins around on a different path. ★

Neptune's orbit

Sun

Earth's orbit

Pluto's orbit

Kuiper Belt

The Kuiper Belt

Beyond Pluto lies a huge ring of frozen rocks known as the Kuiper Belt. Some astronomers think a few of these rocks may be bigger than Pluto.

The loose, drifting rocks of the Kuiper Belt did not merge into one of the planets, when the Solar System was formed.

Oort Cloud

Even farther away sits a huge misty cloud, which may be made up of trillions of comets. This is called the Oort Cloud.

The Oort Cloud surrounds the outer edge of the Solar System like a vast, dusty ball.

Solar System

43

Bits and pieces

Our Solar System isn't just the Sun, the nine planets, and their moons. There are countless asteroids, meteoroids and comets flying around in it too.

The Asteroid Belt. Some asteroids are barely bigger than boulders.

Asteroids

Asteroids are lumps of rocks and metal. Between Mars and Jupiter lies a large band of them, called the Asteroid Belt. The biggest one is called Ceres and is nearly 975km (605 miles) across. Some asteroids even have their own little moons.

Meteoroids

Meteoroids are smaller pieces of rock from space. Most are no bigger than a grain of instant coffee, but some are the size of large rocks. Most burn up in the atmosphere as they fall to Earth, but some are too big to burn, and cause damage when they reach Earth.

Meteoroids that burn up in the sky are called meteors or shooting stars.

This crater in Arizona, USA, was caused by a meteoroid.

Go to **www.usborne-quicklinks.com** and type in the keywords "first space" for a link to a Web site with amazing photographs of comets, asteroids and meteorites.

Comets

Comets are large balls of ice and dust. They come in from the outer edge of the Solar System to circle the Sun. Once past Jupiter, the heat from the Sun begins to melt the outer layer of the comet, and the solar wind blows a trail of gas and dust behind it.

A comet far away ★ from the Sun has no tail. It is just a solid block of dirty ice.

★

Part of the Bayeux Tapestry shows people looking at a comet in 1066.

The picture below shows the Comet Hale-Bopp when it passed by the Earth in 1997.

Closer to the Sun, ★ the outside begins to melt, and forms a trail of gas and dust.

By the time it flies ★ by the Earth the comet's tail is glowing. This makes the comet easy to spot.

The Universe

The Universe is everything in space. It is impossible to imagine how huge it is. Scientists think it is getting bigger all the time, so we will never be able to see to the very edge of space.

Light years

Space is so big that distances are hard to understand if you use normal measurements. Because of this, scientists describe space distances in "light years". One light year is the distance that lights travels in one year.

A journey across the Universe

These pictures show what you would see if you could travel across the Universe in a spaceship. Start on the Earth (at the bottom of this page) and follow the numbers.

(2) Here you reach the edge of our galaxy, the Milky Way, 90,000 light years away.

(1) When you had passed the Moon and planets, you would reach the nearest stars, over four light years away.

Planets

The Moon

Earth

START

Go to **www.usborne-quicklinks.com** and type in the keywords "first space" for a link to a Web site where you can watch a movie about the Big Bang.

The speed of light

The fastest thing in the Universe is light. It takes 1.3 seconds to get from the Moon to Earth, and 8.5 minutes to get from the Sun to Earth.

③ This is the Andromeda Galaxy, the nearest large galaxy to the Milky Way. It is 2.5 million light years away.

The Big Bang

Most scientists think the Universe began with a huge explosion, which they call the Big Bang. Here is what might have happened.

15 billion years ago ★ there was a massive explosion. Inside it, all the material in the Universe was created in an instant.

★
As the explosion cooled, swirling gas clouds collected in clumps. Inside, stars began to form.

The clouds gathered to make galaxies. Five billion years ago our Sun and Solar System began to form.

④ Galaxies group together in clusters. Ours is part of a group called The Local Cluster.

⑤ Farther out, clusters of galaxies revolve around other clusters. They make huge groups called superclusters.

Distant suns

When you look up at the stars in the night sky you are actually seeing millions of distant suns. Stars only look tiny because they are so far away.

How big are stars?

Stars vary in size a lot. Here is how some other stars compare with our own star, the Sun.

Sun

Aldebaran

Rigel

Arcturus

Barnard's star

Star shades

Not all stars are white, although it is difficult to see this by just looking at the night sky. Some are red, or yellow or blue. You can see these differences much more easily in a photograph.

Below you can see stars in a part of the sky called the Sagittarius constellation.

White or blue stars are usually very bright and very hot.

Yellow stars, like our Sun, are usually cooler than white or blue stars.

Some of the largest stars are red. Compared to other stars they are cool.

Go to **www.usborne-quicklinks.com** and type in the keywords "first space" for a link to a Web site with descriptions of different kinds of stars.

Star clusters

Stars may look like they are scattered throughout the sky, but they hang together in clusters. This is because new stars are usually formed in groups, rather than singly. There are two main types of star clusters – open clusters and globular clusters.

This star formation is an open cluster. Stars in open clusters are usually bright and young.

The star formation below is a globular cluster. The stars here are older, and are gathered together more tightly than stars in an open cluster. Globular clusters can contain up to a million stars.

A star's life

Stars are born, they shine, and eventually they die. Every stage of a star's life takes many millions of years.

Stars are being born here, at the top of this column of dust.

Birth of a star

Stars are formed in a vast, swirling cloud of gas and dust called a nebula. You can see part of one here, called the Eagle Nebula. Below you can see how a star forms in a nebula.

1. Inside the nebula, clouds of gas form into dense clumps.

2. These clumps collapse inward to form a core which will become a star.

3. The core grows hotter and hotter.

4. The hot gas starts to explode, and the core begins to shine.

A middle-sized star, like our Sun, will shine for 10 billion years. Smaller stars shine for longer. Massive stars shine very brightly, but burn out quicker.

The Eagle Nebula is so big it would take a ray of light a whole year to cross the area shown in this picture.

Death of a star

Eventually, a star's supply of gas runs out and it dies. This is what will happen to our Sun in around five billion years time.

1. Our Sun will become a Red Giant. This means it will swell up and turn red.

2. Gas on the outside will burn off into space.

3. A very heavy and much smaller ball, called a white dwarf, will be left.

4. The white dwarf will cool and fade away.

Supernovas

When stars much bigger than our Sun reach the end of their life, they explode. These explosions are called supernovas. Only four of them have been seen from Earth in the last thousand years.

This dying star is the Hourglass Nebula. Rings of gas are blowing away from it.

Go to **www.usborne-quicklinks.com** and type in the keywords "first space" for a link to a Web site with amazing facts about stars and a quiz to test your knowledge.

Galaxies

Galaxies are collections of billions of stars, held together by gravity in one vast group. Most galaxies have a spiral shape, but some have a more scattered pattern. There are billions of galaxies in the Universe.

The Milky Way

The Sun is part of a galaxy called the Milky Way. It has over 100 billion stars, and is about 100,000 light years across. The Milky Way is not the biggest galaxy in the Universe, but it is much larger than many others. Like most galaxies it is spinning around a central hub. ★

Astronomers think the Sun and our Solar System are here.

A long trip

It takes 225 million years for the Milky Way to go all the way around. The last time our Solar System was in the same place in space that it is now, dinosaurs roamed the Earth.

If you could see the Milky Way from the side, it would look like a flat plate with a bulge in the middle.

The middle of the Milky Way is hidden by great clouds of dust.

Go to **www.usborne-quicklinks.com** and type in the keywords "first space" for a link to a Web site where you can discover why our galaxy is known as the Milky Way and what other galaxies can be seen from Earth.

Galaxy shapes

Not all galaxies look like the Milky Way. There are several other galaxy shapes. You can see three of them on the right.

This type is known as an irregular galaxy. It doesn't have any real shape at all. ★

This round type is called an elliptical galaxy. ★

This type is a barred spiral galaxy. ★

Radio view

A radio telescope can "see" the Milky Way much more clearly than a telescope. The picture below shows the big bulge in the middle of our galaxy.

The red patch in this picture shows where most of the stars are in the Milky Way.

How many galaxies?

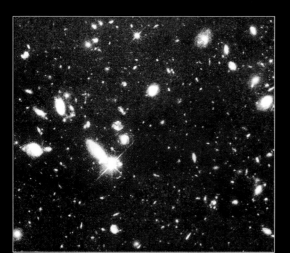

A hundred years ago astronomers thought the Milky Way was the only galaxy in the Universe. But over the last century, telescopes and radio telescopes have detected many millions of other galaxies.

This photo shows newly discovered galaxies. Before this picture was taken, astronomers thought there was nothing in this part of space.

Weird and wonderful

Far, far away in the depths of space, stars and galaxies are behaving in strange and amazing ways. Scientists have only recently invented telescopes and radio telescopes powerful enough to see such things.

This is a painting of what astronomers think a black hole looks like. It is sucking in everything around it.

A typical black hole is about the size of a town.

Everything near a black hole swirls around it, before it is sucked in.

A jet of super hot gas shoots out above and below the black hole.

Black holes

When some very big stars die, instead of fading away, they collapse in on themselves. Everything the star is made of packs down into a very dense ball called a black hole. The gravity of this ball is so strong everything around it, including light, is sucked into it. Black holes are invisible, but what goes on around them shows us where they are.

Go to **www.usborne-quicklinks.com** and type in the keywords "first space" for a link to a Web site where you can find out more about how scientists are able to study black holes.

Cosmic chaos

Everything in space is moving, and sometimes entire galaxies cross each other's path. The photograph on the right, shows two galaxies, named the Antennae Galaxies, colliding. It takes millions of years for one galaxy to pass through another.

Cartwheel Galaxy

The picture on the left shows what a galaxy looks like after it has collided with another galaxy. Astronomers call this one the Cartwheel Galaxy, because a vast wheel-like circle of new stars has formed around its edge.

Spinners

Sometimes a collapsing star makes a pulsar, rather than a black hole. As it shrinks, it spins faster and faster and becomes so dense, a piece the size of a sugar cube would weigh a billion tonnes (tons).

As a pulsar spins, it gives off waves, or pulses, of tiny specks called electrons. These can be picked up by radio telescopes. The pulsar looks like it is flashing on and off.

There is a pulsar in the Crab Nebula.

You can see it here, flashing.

Alien signals?

When scientists first detected pulsars they thought they had made contact with aliens. The regular beeps they picked up on a radio telescope sounded like messages from outer space.

Radio telescopes

Spiral galaxy

Looking at the night sky

Although many of the pictures in this book were taken using very powerful telescopes, you can still see many amazing things in the night sky just with your eyes.

Milky Way

The Moon

Star cluster. This one is called the Hyades.

The Moon

The clearest sight in the night sky is the Moon. You can see it glowing brightly in the darkness because it is lit up by light from the Sun. As the Moon orbits the Earth it seems to change shape.

Old star. This one is called Betelgeuse.

This group of stars is called Orion.

This star is called Sirius. It is the brightest star in the sky.

New Moon
When no light shines on the Moon, it is impossible to see it.

Waxing Moon
Gradually a sliver of light returns. The Moon appears to grow.

Full Moon
Once every 28 days all of one side of the Moon is lit by the Sun's light.

What you can see

There is a lot to see in the night sky, if you know what to look for. The picture above shows some of the things you can see without a telescope, which you can find out about in this book.

Waning Moon
As the Moon moves in its orbit less light falls on it. It seems to shrink.

Go to **www.usborne-quicklinks.com** and type in the keywords "first space" for a link to a Web site on astronomy.

Stars

A clear night sky is full of stars. There are certain patterns you can look for. These patterns are called constellations, and there are 88 altogether.

This is a star pattern called Orion, which you can also see on the left-hand page. Ancient people thought this shape looked like a hunter.

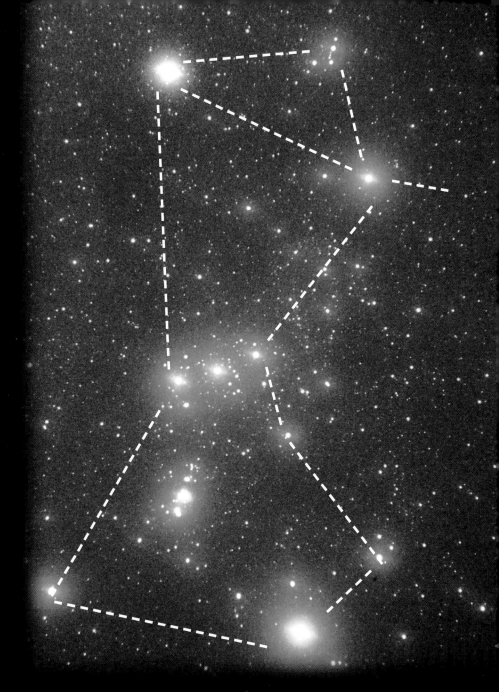

This is a photo of the constellation of Orion.

The Milky Way

You can see the Milky Way at certain times of the year if you are away from city lights, and the night sky is clear. It looks like a thick band of faint stars splashed across the sky like spilled milk.

This photo shows what the Milky Way looks like on a very clear night.

Binoculars and telescopes

You can see plenty of things in the night sky with just your eyes, but you can see a lot more with binoculars or a telescope.

Binoculars

A good pair of binoculars is cheaper than a telescope. Binoculars are great for skywatching because they are light and easy to aim at the things in the sky that you want to look at.

This picture shows what a star cluster and three single stars look like through binoculars.

You use this focus wheel to make the image you are looking at sharper.

You hold on to the binoculars here.

Moon watching

Try looking at the Moon with your binoculars or with a telescope. You can see mountains, craters and flat "seas". Sunlight casts long shadows.

You look through these eyepieces. You can turn them to make the object you are looking at clearer.

FULLY COATED
36ft / 1000yds
12m / 1000m
Field 7°

Binoculars have two front lenses – one for each eyepiece.

Go to www.usborne-quicklinks.com and type in the keywords "first space" for a link to a Web site with useful advice on buying binoculars and telescopes.

Telescopes

Telescopes make things look much bigger than binoculars can. It's not worth buying a cheap telescope though. If you don't have a lot of money to spend, binoculars are a much better buy.

Here is the same star cluster and three single stars that you can also see on the facing page. A telescope makes them look bigger.

Telescope tube

Most telescopes are heavy, so you will need to put yours on a tripod (stand) to keep it steady. You can see things much more clearly if they don't shake!

This is a small, low power telescope. You use it to find things in the sky before looking at them with the big telescope.

The Andromeda Galaxy, seen with a telescope like the one on this page.

Galaxies

If you know where to look you can even see other galaxies with a telescope. They look like small misty patches of light. One of the easiest to see is the Andromeda Galaxy, which is two and a half million light years away from Earth.

You make your image sharper with this wheel.

This is the viewer for the big telescope.

This three leg stand is called a tripod.

Space words

Here are some important space words which you'll find throughout this book.

alien a living thing from another world.

antenna the part of a radio where radio waves are picked up or sent out.

asteroid a rock orbiting the Sun. Thousands of them can be found in a part of the Solar System called the Asteroid Belt.

astronaut someone who goes into space.

atmosphere layers of gas that surround a planet or a star.

cargo bay area on a spacecraft, such as a space shuttle, where large objects such as satellites or parts of a space station can be carried.

cluster a group of space objects gathered together, such as stars or galaxies.

comet a chunk of dirty ice orbiting the Sun which can form a long tail as it melts. Comets sometimes come close enough to the Earth so that we can see them.

core the middle of a planet, moon, star or other space object.

crater a hollow on the surface of a planet, moon or asteroid, caused by something hitting it, such as a meteorite or asteroid.

day the time it takes a planet or moon to spin all the way around.

galaxy a group of hundreds of millions of stars all held together by gravity.

gravity a force that pulls objects toward other objects. (Usually smaller objects to larger objects.)

laboratory a place where scientists do experiments.

light year the distance a ray of light travels in one Earth year. This is 9,500,000,000,000km (5,900,000, 000,000 miles).

meteor a meteoroid that burns up in a planet's atmosphere. Also called a shooting star.

meteorite a meteoroid that hits the surface of a planet.

meteoroid dust, or small chunks of rock, in orbit around the Sun.

moon a mini-planet in orbit around another planet.

nebula an enormous cloud of gas and dust where new stars can form.

orbit the path of an object in space, as it travels around another object. For example, the Earth is in orbit around the Sun and the Moon is in orbit around the Earth.

planet a huge ball of rock or gas, which travels around a star.

radio telescope a type of telescope which uses radio waves to "see" objects in space. You can see pictures of some radio telescopes on pages 10 –11.

robot a machine that can do a job in a similar way to a person.

rocket a type of engine in a spacecraft which uses exploding fuel to make it move.

satellite 1) something in space which orbits around something else. For example, the Moon is a satellite of Earth. **2)** an unmanned spacecraft which orbits the Earth.

solar panel a metal sheet used to gather heat from the Sun which can then be used to make electricity.

solar system a group of planets, and other objects, all in orbit around a sun. You can see a picture of our Solar System on pages 28 – 29.

solar wind a stream of tiny particles that blow off the Sun's surface and into space. When they pass by the North and South Poles of Earth they make the sky light up.

spacecraft (also called spaceship) a vehicle that is used to travel up to and in space. If a spacecraft has no people in it, it is unmanned.

space probe an unmanned spacecraft which collects information about objects in space.

space station a base in space, used for space exploration. You can see a picture of a space station on pages 18 – 19.

spacewalk when an astronaut in a spacesuit leaves a spacecraft and floats in space.

star a huge ball of exploding gas.

surface the outermost part of a star, planet or other space objects.

Universe everything that exists in space.

weightless when a person or thing in space appears to have no weight, and floats around.

year the length of time it takes a planet to travel around the Sun. Earth's year lasts 365 days.

Index

General Web sites

Go to **www.usborne-quicklinks.com** and type in the keywords "first space" for links to the following Web sites:

Web site 1: Design your own space station and read about astronomers through the ages.
Web site 2: Visit the main NASA Web site, where you can read the latest space news stories, try out online activities and find links to hundreds of other exciting Web sites.
Web site 3: Build a galaxy, test your knowledge of the Solar System with a quiz and find out more about comets by making your own.

Picture credits

The Publishers are grateful to the following for permission to reproduce material:

front and back cover, Digital Vision; spine, Stockbyte; p1, Digital Vision; p2-3 NASA/NSSDC; p4bl, NASA and the Hubble Heritage Team (STSml); p4-5t, Digital Vision; p5tr, NASA/NSSDC; p5br, NOAO/SPL; p6tl, Roger Rossmeyer/CORBIS; p6bm NASA/SOHO/ESA; p7, Digital Vision; p8tr Bettmann/Corbis; p8b, Jim Sugar Photography/Corbis; p9br, NASA; p10l NOAO/STScl/NASA; p10r, Jack O. Burns (University of Missouri) and David Clarke (St Mary's University, Nova Scotia); p10-11, Roger Ressmeyer/Corbis; p12bl, Digital Vision; p12-13, Digital Vision; p13br, NASA; p14, NASA; p15 NASA; p16m, NASA/SPL; p17bl, Digital Vision; p17br, NASA/SPL; p18-19 (background), Digital Vision; p18-19 (foreground), NASA; p20m, CORBIS; p20bl, Digital Vision; p21m, NASA; p21br, David Ducros/SPL; p22l, Digital Vision; p22tl, Genesis Space Photo Library; p22-23, NASA/SOHO/ESA; p23tr, Julian Baum/SPL; p23bl, NASA; p23bm, NASA/SOHO/ESA; p23br, Digital Vision; p24l, NASA/JPL/Malin Space Science System; p24m, NASA/HSFI/Pat Rawlings; p24mb, A. Gragera, Latin Stock/SPL; p25r, Chris Butler/SPL; p26bl, NASA/SPL; p26br, Stephanie Maze/CORBIS; p27tl, Victor Habbick Visions/SPL; p27ml, NASA/JPL; p27bl, NASA/SPL; p28m, Digital Vision; p28br, Digital Vision; p29l, Digital Vision; p29tl, NASA/SOHO/ESA; p29tl, NASA/NSSDC; p29mt, Digital Vision; p29m, NASA/NSSDC; p29ml, Kenneth Seidelman, U.S. Naval Observatory; p29bl, NASA; p29tr, NASA/NSSDC; p29br, Digital Vision; p30l, NASA/U.S. Geological Survey; p30mr, Digital Vision; p31b, Digital Vision; p32bl, NASA/SPL; p NASA/SOHO/ESA; p33mr, NASA/SPL; p33brl, Digital Vision; p33brm, NASA/NSSDC/Viking; p33brr, Digital Vision; p35t, NASA/U.S. Geological Survey; p35b, NASA/JPL; p36l, NASA/JPL/MSSS; p37l, NASA/JPL/Caltech; p37m, NASA/JPL/Caltech; p37r, NASA/JPL/MSSS; p37b, NASA/JPL/MPF; p38ml, NASA/SPL; p38mr, CORBIS; p38br, NASA; p39tm, SPL; p39mr, NASA; p39bm, Astro-geology Team/USGS; p39br, Digital Vision; p40mr, NASA; p40m, JPL/CALTECH/NASA/Calvin J. Hamilton; p40ml, JPL/CALTECH/NASA/Calvin J. Hamilton; p40l, JPL/CALTECH/NASA/Calvin J. Hamilton; p40bl, JPL/CALTECH/NASA/Calvin J. Hamilton; p40bl, JPL/CALTECH/NASA/Calvin J. Hamilton; p40br, NASA; p40-41b, David Hardy/SPL; p41mr, NASA; p44b, John Sanford/SPL; p44l, NASA; p45m, J.Finch/SPL; p46tl, WFI/European Southern Observatory; p46m, Roger Ressmeyer/Corbis; p46b, Digital Vision; p47tl, Digital Vision; p47mr, NASA/Hubble Heritage Project (AURA/STScl); p47br, NASA/A. Fruchter and the ERO Team (STScl, ST-ECF); p48br, Hubble Heritage Team (AURA/STScl /NASA); p49tl, R. Gilmozzi/Hubble/STScl; p 49b, NASA/W. Brandner/E. Grebel/ Y.H. Chu; p50l, Digital Vision; p51r, NASA/JPL/WFPC2; p53bl, Space Telescope Science Institute/NASA/SPL; p53m, Max Planck Institut fur Radioastronomie/SPL; p54ml, David A. Hardy/SPL; p55tr, NASA/Brad Whitmore (STScl); p55m, Digital Vision; p55bm, NASA/Jeff Hester & Paul Scowen; p55br Bettmann/Corbis; p57bl, Gerry Schad/SPL; p57tr, John Sandford/SPL; p58-59, Digital Vision; p58bl, Howard Allman/Broadhurst Clarkson & Fuller Ltd, London; p59 br, Howard Allman/Broadhurst Clarkson & Fuller Ltd, London.

Key
t = top, m = middle, b= bottom, l = left, r = right, SPL = Science Photo Library